EPP

EssexWorks.
...lity of life

WRITTLE

25/11/2019.

D0581228

Please return this book on or before the date shown above. To renew go to www.essex.gov.uk/libraries, ring 0845 603 7628 or go to any Essex library.

Essex County Council

ROBO-RUNNERS

Powerball

by DAMIAN HARVEY

Illustrated by Mark Oliver

Hodder Children's Books

A division of Hachette Children's Books

Hodder Children's Books
A division of Hachette Children's Books
338 Euston Road, London NW1 3BH
An Hachette Livre UK company

For Deanna Harvey
with lots of love

The Iron City stands like a giant metal crab, high in the Mountains of Khan. Its eight legs dig deep into the ground, supporting the main body of the city and giving easy access to the iron mines that lie beneath. Two arms reach up into the air, holding landing platforms for the mining craft and spaceships that buzz around it.

The air is filled with smoke and steam from the many chimneys and cooling towers that cover its back like barnacles. Down below, the valley floor is littered with piles of scragg – compacted waste that's been dumped from the furnaces and work-shops of the city.

Towards this towering city of metal and steam came four robot friends, Crank, Al, Torch and Grunt, travelling in search of a safe place for old robots.

A place where robots can be free to live their lives in peace.

A place called Robotika.

The spacecraft they were travelling in slowly approached the city, waiting for clearance to land on one of the platforms. Every few minutes, the craft rattled as if it were about to fall apart.

Scamp, the botweiler, lowered his head and let out a long whine – even the robo-dog didn't like the way the craft shook.

"Are you sure this thing's safe?" asked Torch, the old Fire and Rescue robot.

"Of course it's safe," said Maximus Bullwart, the pilot of the *Starship Terrapin*. "This craft has flown to the farthest reaches of the galaxy and has never failed me yet."

"You've been to the far reaches of the galaxy?" said Crank. "What's it like?"

"I didn't say I'd been," said Maximus, shaking his head. "I said the *Terrapin* had. It used to be a great starship but now it's got too many holes in it to fly into outer space. I just use it to get around the planet and scout for new players."

Maximus Bullwart was the head scout for the world-famous powerball team – the Iron City Eagles. He'd been waiting outside the coliseum when Crank, Al, Torch and Grunt had escaped from the gladiator robots and the deadly Razorbites. Maximus had told the four friends that they would make excellent powerball players.

Crank had thought this sounded great – they would all be famous – but the others weren't so sure.

"We don't want to be famous," said Torch. "We just want to get to Robotika where we'll be safe."

"Nonsense," cried Maximus. "Everyone wants to be famous, and after what I saw you guys do at the coliseum I can tell that you'll be big … REALLY BIG. I bet you could be the best powerball players in the galaxy."

"In the whole galaxy?" said Crank, sounding amazed. "This could be even *better* than finding Robotika."

"But we have never played powerball in our lives," said Al. "We could get hurt."

"Don't you worry," said Maximus. "The coach will teach you everything you need to know. You'll be stars in no time."

"See," said Crank. "There's nothing to worry about … We're going to be stars."

Crank had seen powerball games on the vid-screens when he'd lived in Metrocity. It was a fast, furious and exciting sport. The fans loved it and the players were treated like heroes. Crank could see it now … crowds of screaming fans waiting to get a vid-snap of him at the end of each game. It would be fantastic.

A loud beep from the *Terrapin*'s control panel brought Crank back from his daydreaming, and a crackly voice came over the loudspeakers giving them instructions to land.

"Hold tight," said Maximus. "We're going in."

As Maximus Bullwart pulled on the flight stick

and steered the *Starship Terrapin* towards the nearest landing pad, the others watched in wonder as the Iron City filled the display screen in front of them.

The four friends had all heard about the Iron City before. Even Al, who was a new robot, had heard tales of the moving city that walked through the Mountains of Khan.

They had heard of its iron walls and steel floors, its towering chimneys and its maze of walkways that shone like polished silver. They'd

heard about the teams of robots that constantly worked on the city, cleaning and repairing it so that it stayed in perfect working order.

The Iron City was a marvel of modern engineering. The perfect mining city. Whenever the mines ran dry, the whole city would just move on and find another place to dig.

None of them had ever dreamed they would visit the Iron City but now they were approaching it, it wasn't quite the way they had expected it to be.

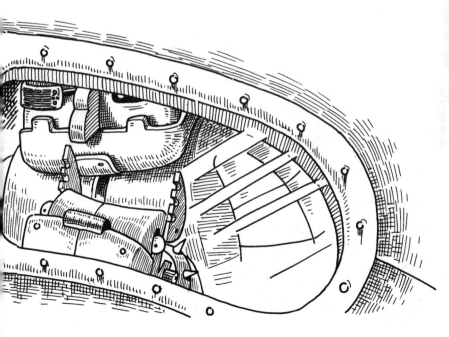

Instead of being made of shining, polished metal, the city looked old and rusty. Some of the walkways were damaged and broken, and many of the chimneys were battered and bent out of shape. Most of the windows seemed to be covered in thick layers of dust and grime and some of them were broken or missing completely. Through the window of the *Starship Terrapin* it looked as though the Iron City was falling apart.

There was a gentle bump as Maximus landed the *Terrapin* on the platform and then a sudden jolt as it jerked forwards before coming to a complete stop. Crank, Al, Torch and Grunt went flying into one of the walls and Scamp, the botweiler, growled as he slid across the floor towards them.

"Sorry about the bumpy landing," said Maximus. "It always does that after touching down."

"*Now* he tells us," complained Torch, picking himself up off the floor.

"It's nothing," said Crank. "Just wait until we get out of here and see all the fans."

"Fans?" said Al. "What fans?"

"We're Iron City Eagles now," said Crank excitedly. "There's bound to be crowds of fans."

As Crank eagerly made his way towards the boarding ramp Al, Torch and Grunt looked at each other and shrugged.

They were getting used to Crank, and the way he sometimes let his excitement get the better of him.

The boarding ramp at the back of the *Terrapin* dropped open with a crash and Crank slowly made his way off the craft, waving his hands at the crowd of fans … then he stopped and screamed.

2

As Crank screamed, Torch, Al and Grunt raced down the boarding ramp to see what was wrong. Scamp, the botweiler, leaped down beside them, baring his steely claws and gnashing his teeth.

"What is it?" asked Torch looking round eagerly. "What's wrong?"

Crank gazed around the landing pad and shook his head in disbelief. "Where are they all?" he asked.

"Where's who?" said Maximus, as he joined Crank and the others.

"The fans!" said Crank. "Where are all the fans?"

"What fans?" said Maximus Bullwart, looking puzzled. "Oh … you mean the powerball fans."

"Of course," said Crank. "I thought they'd all be here cheering for us."

"They will be," said Maximus. "But you're not stars yet. Just wait until you've had your first game. The fans will be chasing you all over the city."

"Is that all it was?" said Torch, relaxing. "I thought you were in danger."

"Danger?" said Crank. "It was worse than danger. I must have looked ridiculous … I was waving at nothing."

"Never mind," said Maximus, giving Crank a friendly pat on the shoulder. "We'll take a shuttle pod down to the city and I'll show you round."

The four friends joined Maximus as he headed for the shuttle tube with Scamp following close behind, but as they made their way across the landing pad a loud voice shouted out after them.

"Oi!" yelled the voice. "You can't bring that thing into the city."

The friends looked round and saw a miserable-looking robot with a clipboard in its hand, pointing at Scamp.

"That isn't a *fing*," said Grunt. "It's Scamp, and he goes everywhere dat I go."

"Well that's easy then," said the robot, smiling at Grunt. "You're not going into the city either."

"But we are Iron City Eagles," said Crank.

"We are going to be powerball stars."

"That's right," said Maximus, stepping forward to talk to the miserable-looking robot. "And this robo-dog is our new mascot."

The robot threw its head back and laughed. "Iron City Eagles!" it cried. "What a load of scragg. You'd better take this robo-mutt with you then. You'll need all the help you can get."

"Dat robot is askin' for trouble," growled Grunt.

"You don't want to upset the space traffic wardens," said Maximus. "They can get quite nasty when they get upset."

"Dey will be more dan upset when I 'ave finished with dem," growled Grunt as he followed the others.

"And you'd better not leave this pile of junk here for long either," shouted the space traffic warden, walking towards the *Starship Terrapin*.

"Wot is you gonna do about it?" grumbled Grunt.

"I'll have it taken away and crushed," said the robot. "That's what I'll do."

Before the space traffic warden disappeared, it gave the *Starship Terrapin* a kick, sending a shower of rust and flaking paint tumbling to the floor.

Crank and the others hadn't had a chance to get a good look at the outside of the *Terrapin* before. When they'd dived on board, outside the coliseum, they were being chased by vicious Razorbites – flying insect-like robots with razor-sharp claws and teeth. But now that they had time to look, they could see that the space traffic warden was right. The *Starship Terrapin* was a pile of junk.

The *Terrapin* was bashed and dented, with more holes in it than the emperor of Jupiter's hat. To decorate it, the words *Iron City Eagles* had been written across the side in splashes of bright yellow paint.

"It *does* look like a pile of junk," whispered Al. "I cannot believe we actually flew in that thing."

"Well, people thought we were junk, didn't they," said Crank. "But we're not."

Torch nodded in agreement. It wasn't long ago that they'd all been treated like pieces of worthless junk and sent to the recycling plant to be crushed. Al had even had his legs pulled off and he was still having to walk around on his hands. The very thought of the place made their joints rattle with fear.

Maximus led the four friends to one of the shuttle tubes that stood in the middle of the landing platform. Two of the tubes were already being used but the third one held a shuttle pod.

"It'll be a bit of a squeeze," said Maximus, as the shuttle

pod's door slid open. "But I'm sure we'll all fit in."

The pod was shaped like an egg, with windows and a row of seats inside.

While Crank and the others squeezed themselves into the seats, Maximus closed the door and fastened his safety belt.

"You should fasten your belts too," said Maximus. "The shuttle pods are very fast."

"Don't you worry about us," said Crank, nodding his head and smiling. "We're used to going fast. We've driven high-powered tunnel racers beneath the junk yards of Metrocity. We've hurtled across the Wastelands at speeds you wouldn't—"

But before Crank had time to finish what he was saying the shuttle pod shot forwards, forcing the robots back into their seats.

"Aieeeee!" squealed Crank as the pod hurtled into the shuttle tube and dropped down towards the main body of the city.

Through the windows, everything was a blur as the pod picked up speed, rattled round tight corners and bumped over joints in the tube.

Al flew out of his seat and was sent crashing against the back of the pod. Grunt bashed his head against one of the side windows, cracking the glass, and Torch accidentally fired a jet of flame from his wrist nozzle, melting the seat next to him and filling the pod with thick, black smoke.

When they had been built, the shuttle pods had been fitted with comfortable seating and bright lights so that passengers could relax as they whizzed from one side of the Iron City to the other. But now, the seating was battered and worn and the lights flickered every time the shuttle pod went round a bend or hit a bump.

Only Scamp, sitting with his head hanging out of the window, seemed to be enjoying the journey.

Crank's fingers gripped the safety rail in front of him as he desperately tried to stop himself

from bouncing out of his seat.

"Stop …!" he cried. "I WANT TO GET OFF."

Then as quickly as it had started … the shuttle
pod stopped, and the four robots flew forwards
out of their seats.

"Here we are," said Maximus Bullwart. "The
magnificent Iron City."

The shuttle pod's door slid open and Crank, Al, Torch and Grunt staggered out in a cloud of smoke. They found themselves in a large hallway bustling with robots of all shapes and sizes. Vid-screens hung from the walls, giving news about what was going on in the Iron City.

"Look," said Crank. "The Iron City Eagles are playing tomorrow night."

The four friends barely had time to look at the screen before being pushed out of the way.

"Do you mind?" said Al, as three small robots shoved past and disappeared into the shuttle pod behind him. "There is no need to push."

There was a loud hissing sound from inside the shuttle pod and a wall of white foam gushed out of the door and bubbled across the floor.

Then, as quickly as they had arrived, the three small robots charged out of the pod and disappeared from view.

"What was all that about?" asked Crank.

A figure emerged from the shuttle pod wiping foam from its face. "They," said Maximus Bullwart, flicking the foam on to the floor, "are the fire drones. They must have been alerted by all the smoke in the shuttle pod."

"But the fire was already out," said Torch.

Maximus nodded in agreement. "The drones are very keen," he said, "but not very clever. Come on," he continued. "I'll take you up to the Eagles' Nest."

"The Eagles' Nest!" said Crank. "What in the world is that?"

"It's the powerball dome where the Iron City Eagles play. We call it the Eagles' Nest."

"Great," said Crank enthusiastically. "We can't wait."

Al, Torch and Grunt weren't quite as enthusiastic as Crank but they still followed, making their way across the busy hallway to a row of lift doors.

There was a loud squeak and grinding of gears

as the lift doors slowly opened, and the four friends looked at each other.

"Could we please use the stairs?" asked Al. "I think we have had enough of shuttle tubes and rickety spacecraft."

"Don't you worry," said Maximus. "The lifts in the Iron City are perfectly safe."

Reluctantly, the four friends followed Maximus into the lift, which groaned under their weight.

Then, as the lift doors started to close behind them, a big foam-covered shape came charging through the crowd.

Robots jumped and dived out of the way and the shape leaped between the lift doors just before they closed completely.

"Allo Scamp," said Grunt, patting the robo-dog's foam-covered head.

The lift squeaked and shuddered under the extra weight and a terrible groaning sound could be heard from the shaft above them.

"Keep still," cried Crank. "You're rocking the lift."

"Don't worry," said Maximus. "These lifts have been running for over a hundred years and we've never had a problem with them yet."

"Oh great," groaned Crank. "Now we're riding in an ancient lift. This place just gets better by the minute."

As the lift went up it rattled and shook, and the

four friends could hear the steel cables clattering and echoing in the shaft above them. Eventually they came to a juddering halt and the doors slowly opened to reveal a dimly lit passageway. Pipes lined the walls on both sides and jets of steam hissed from taps and joints.

"Well this looks nice," said Al.

"It's a shortcut," said Maximus, stepping out of the lift and disappearing through a cloud of steam.

As the four friends hurried to keep up, there was a noise from the lift behind them. Torch turned to see Scamp, the botweiler, jumping out of the lift as it gave another loud groan. The loud groan was followed by an even louder crack and squeal of metal as the lift suddenly dropped – plummeting into the darkness of the shaft below.

"Oh dear," said Maximus, shaking his head as he reappeared. "That's never happened before. But don't worry ... there's another lift we can use later."

"Another lift!" cried Crank. "No thank you ...

Next time we *definitely* use the stairs."

"You *really* don't want to be using the stairs," said Maximus, shaking his head again. "The stairs aren't safe at all."

Before any of the others had the chance to say anything, Maximus came to an abrupt halt. In front of him was a curved door with a large locking wheel at its centre. Gripping the wheel in both hands, Maximus grunted and strained, turning the wheel until the door slowly opened.

"Here we are," said Maximus, climbing through the doorway.

The four friends followed him into what seemed to be a large room.

"What is it?" asked Grunt.

"This," said Maximus proudly, "is the Eagles' Nest."

"It's a bit gloomy," said Torch.

"The Eagles' Nest is solar-powered," said Maximus. "During the day the sun shines through the glass roof and charges everything up so that we can even play games when it's dark."

"But it's daytime now," said Torch, "and I can't see the sun."

"That's because the roof's so dirty," said Maximus sadly. "A team of robots used to clean the roof every week, but the Iron City Eagles aren't as rich as they used to be and we've had to make a few cut-backs."

"Cut-backs!" said Crank. "What sort of cut-backs?"

"Oh, nothing important," said Maximus. "Just a little bit here and a little bit there. Nothing anyone would notice. Now the roof gets cleaned just before we have a game … but the most important thing is we've still got a team … and the Iron City Eagles are the best powerball team in the galaxy. Now follow me," Maximus continued. "It's time to meet the rest of the Iron City Eagles."

As Maximus led them across the room, Torch switched on his lamp so they could get a better look at the powerball dome. "Just look at the place," he said. "It's enormous."

Torch moved his lamp around so they could all get a good look. The Eagles' Nest was big and round. The roof was glass but the walls and floor looked like smooth, polished metal. It was like standing inside a giant ball bearing.

"When everything is powered up the walls glow and become almost transparent," said Maximus. "It means the fans can sit and watch the game without getting injured."

"What are those things?" asked Al, pointing up at two funnels that curled down from the roof.

"They are the goals," said Maximus. "Put the ball in there and you score a point."

Directly beneath the goal funnels was a flat, circular piece of flooring.

"I've seen *this* on the vid-screens," said Crank excitedly, stepping into the circle. "This is where the players get into the arena."

"That's right," said Maximus. "And this is also how we get down to the team room."

As soon as the four friends were standing beneath the goal funnels, the floor started to sink – taking them down beneath the powerball dome.

"This is the team room," said Maximus proudly. "And this is Avatar … the Captain of the Iron City Eagles. I'll tell the coach you're here while you all get to know each other."

Avatar smiled and nodded her head at the four friends. Behind her stood another of the Iron City Eagles, but Crank barely noticed it at all. He just stood and stared at the Captain … his mouth open wide.

Avatar was the most beautiful robot Crank had ever seen in his life.

"It's good to have you on the team," said Avatar, smiling at the four friends. "We need some new players."

"Huh!" growled the other Iron City Eagle behind her – a big old robot with dents and scratches all over his head and body. He glared at Crank and the others for a moment before shaking his head in disgust.

"What we need are *real* players," he said. "Not a bunch of tin cans that have never even *seen* a powerball game."

"I've *seen* lots of powerball games," said Crank, huffily.

"Yes," said Al. "And I have *heard* all about them too."

"You've *heard* about them?" cried the big robot. "*Oh well ... there's nothing for us to worry about then, is there?*"

"All right, Flint. That's enough," said Avatar. "I'm sure they'll do their best."

"Yeah, well," said Flint, scowling. "Let's just hope that their best is good enough."

"How hard can it be?" asked Al. "Maximus said that if you can catch a ball you can play powerball."

"That's right," added Crank. "And Maximus said we've got what it takes to be the best powerball players in the galaxy."

"OH HE DID, DID HE?" roared Flint. "THE BEST IN THE GALAXY?"

The big robot turned away from the four friends and punched one of the metal lockers that stood against the wall next to him.

There was a deafening crash as his fist tore through the locker door and then a screech of tearing metal as he pulled it back out again.

In his hand, Flint was gripping a metal ball.

"Let's see you catch this then, shall we," said Flint, and hurled the ball at Crank.

Crank's eyes opened wide in horror as the metal ball came straight towards his head – then there was a blur in front of his face as Avatar reached out and caught it.

"Flint Armstrong!" said Avatar, shaking her head as she tossed the ball into the air and caught it again. "You must be getting slow in your old age."

Flint grunted in reply and turned to walk away.

"FLINT ARMSTRONG?" cried Crank. "*You're* Flint Armstrong?"

Flint stopped and looked suspiciously at Crank and the others. "What if I am?" he said.

"But you're amazing!" said Crank. "The best powerball player ever."

"Yeah ... well," said Flint, looking at his feet. "I'm not too bad, I suppose."

"Not too bad!" said Crank. "You're brilliant."

"Well ... I wouldn't say that," said Flint.

"Nonsense," interrupted Crank. "I saw you play with the Metrocity Dynamos. Three hundred and fifty-four goals in one championship … You were on fire."

"Well," admitted Flint, smiling, "I suppose I was a bit brilliant."

"All right, all right," said Avatar. "I think we've all agreed that Flint is brilliant so why don't we get out there and have a practice."

"A practice?" said Al. "But we have only just arrived."

"Oh dear," said Flint, quickly going back to his grumpy-sounding self again. "Has the little robot had a busy day then?"

Avatar gave Flint a hard stare that stopped him from saying anything else. "I'm afraid we do have to practise," she said. "We've got a game tomorrow and you need to know what to do."

"Tomorrow?" said Torch. "But we've never even played before."

Flint let out a loud groan and started bashing his head against one of the metal lockers.

"Just ignore him," said Avatar. "Flint gets a bit emotional sometimes."

"Tomorrow does seem a little bit soon for *us* to be having a game," said Al.

"Yes," agreed Avatar, "it is a bit soon, but there's nothing we can do about it. If we don't play we get kicked out of the powerball league. And that will be the end of the Iron City Eagles ... the team will be terminated."

"I am sure it will not be that bad," said Al. "You will not be terminated for losing a game."

"We will," said Avatar. "We'll all be out of a job and there is no place in the Iron City for robots that don't have a job. We'll be on the scrap heap."

"Well, what are we waiting for?" said Crank. "Let's get some practice in before the rest of the team arrive."

"The rest of the team?" said Avatar, looking puzzled. "We are the rest of the team."

"Just two of you?" said Torch.

Avatar nodded. "It's been a rough season," she said. "Beck and Sol were evaporated in last week's game against the New Atlanteans."

"And Saul lost his head when we played the Moonbase Marauders," explained Flint. "That was a right mess ... wires and circuits everywhere."

"Wait a minute," said Crank, "no one said anything about losing our heads."

"Or about being evaporated," said Torch.

"Don't worry," said Avatar. "That sort of thing doesn't happen very often."

"That's right," said Flint, with a wicked grin. "You only lose your head or get evaporated once in your life."

"Well that is *very* reassuring," said Al.

"You'll be fine," said Avatar, giving Flint another one of her icy looks. "Let's get you kitted out so we can get a bit of practice in. The coach will be waiting for us."

"Yeah," said Grunt. "Dat sounds like a good idea

to me. Maximus said dat da coach will tell us everything we need to know."

Avatar rooted in one of the lockers and brought out something that looked like a tangle of wires and thin, metal bones.

"Here," she said, tossing it to Crank. "Try this on."

"What on earth is it?" asked Crank, holding the thing up in the air to examine it.

"It's a power-glove," explained Avatar.

"What do you do with it?" asked Crank.

"It's a glove," said Flint. "It goes on your hand. What do you *think* you do with it?"

"It's not *just* a glove," said Avatar, passing one each to Al, Grunt and Torch. "It's a power-glove."

"It doesn't look very powerful," said Crank.

"Here," said Flint, shaking his head and grabbing hold of Crank's arm. "You've got to switch it on first."

Flint gripped Crank's arm in one hand and twisted the cuff of the power-glove with the other.

The air was filled with a high-pitched hum as the glove powered up.

The wires and metal of the glove vibrated and rattled on Crank's hand and he watched as it slowly knitted itself together.

"Argghhh!" he cried, grabbing his wrist. "Get it off … It's crushing my hand."

While Crank fell to the floor clutching his hand, Grunt grabbed hold of Flint and lifted him into the air.

"What 'ave you done to my friend?" roared Grunt, giving Flint a shake.

Flint desperately tried to free himself from Grunt's grip, but it was no use.

"I was only tightening his power-glove," squeaked Flint.

"Well I fink you had better un-tighten it then, unless you wants me to un-tighten your head from your body," said Grunt.

"It's all right," said Avatar. "Crank will be fine.

Power-gloves only tighten to fit your hand."

Grunt looked at Avatar and soon realised she was telling the truth when he saw Crank back on his feet and looking very embarrassed.

"Oh! Right," said Grunt, letting go of Flint. "Sorry about dat."

"It's all right," said Flint, holding his neck joints. "But with strength like that I think you would be good in defence."

"Defence?" said Grunt, suspiciously. "What's dat?"

"It means your job will be to stop the other team keeping the ball," said Flint.

"Dat's easy," said Grunt. "Grunt will not let dem touch da ball."

"Good," said Avatar. "Now let's go up to the dome. The coach will be waiting for us."

When they reached the dome they found that a pale glow was radiating from the walls, casting a dim light over everything. At one side of the room was a figure in a bright yellow jacket, standing with its back to them. On the back of the jacket they could just make out the Iron City Eagles team logo – a shining powerball gripped in the talons of a giant eagle.

"This is Max," said Avatar. "The head coach."

The head coach turned to face them and smiled, nodding his head in approval.

"I'd heard we had some new players," said the coach, "and you guys look just fine. Now let's get started, shall we?"

Crank, Al, Torch and Grunt just stared.

"But you're Maximus?" said Crank.

"Me?" said the coach. "Of course I'm not … I'm Max, the head coach. See … I've got a whistle and a coach's jacket."

"But you *do* look like Maximus Bullwart," said Crank.

"You look *incredibly* like him," said Torch. "In fact—"

"Why don't we just get started," interrupted

Avatar, picking a metal ball up from the floor by her feet.

The ball was about the size of a melon. Bigger than the one that Flint had thrown at Crank but just small enough to be gripped in one hand. A deep groove ran around the outside of the ball, dividing it into two halves. On one side of the groove the ball was polished and shiny,  whilst on the other it was dark and dull.

"This is a powerball," said Max, tossing the ball into the air. "Now let's see one of you catch it."

The four friends watched as the powerball arced high into the air and then dropped down towards them.

The ball hit the floor with a heavy crack and Flint groaned and slapped his hand against his forehead. "You were supposed to catch it," he said. "What happened?"

"I thought *they* were going to catch it," said Crank.

"Well I fought *you* woz gonna catch it," said Grunt.

"Let's try again," said Max, patiently. "And this time ... *one* of you catch it."

Max picked the ball up again and tossed it into the air.

This time, as it fell towards the four friends, Grunt reached out and grabbed it.

"Hey," cried Crank. "*I* was going to catch it that time."

"It doesn't matter *who* catches it," shouted Max, beginning to lose his temper. "As long as *one* of you does. Now why don't you practise throwing it to each other."

While Scamp sat and watched with interest, the four friends spread out around the arena and threw the ball back and forth for a while. Once they'd got used to that, Max had them running and jumping whilst passing the ball at the same time.

Next came scoring, and the four friends took turns at throwing the metal ball up into the goal funnel. They soon discovered the ball didn't need to be thrown too hard, as once it got close enough to the mouth of the funnel it was sucked up with a THUB before being fired back into play from the top.

"Be careful not to throw it into the wrong funnel," said Max. "Or it will be a point to the other team."

Crank, Torch and Grunt were finding this easy, but Al was having trouble standing on one hand whilst throwing and catching.

"I think it's time to try the anti-grav belt," said Avatar, fastening a thick metal belt around Al's waist.

"Your job will be to guard our goal funnel ... and this belt should make it easier for you."

When she'd finished fastening the belt, Avatar stepped back and nodded. "Why not start it up and see how it goes? But be careful. They can be a bit tricky."

There were two buttons on the anti-grav belt, on and off. Between them was a small dial with little markings on it.

"It looks simple enough," said Al, as he pressed the on button and waited for something to happen.

"Try tapping it," said Avatar.

Al gave the belt a gentle tap but still nothing happened. He poked and prodded at the button a few more times and then gave the dial a twist. As the dial turned the belt let out a high-pitched whine which got louder the more he turned it. But nothing else happened.

Al frowned at the belt and gave it a thump with his hand.

The belt let out a loud popping sound and, with a screech, Al shot into the air like a rocket. This was followed by a loud THUB as his head stuck in the goal funnel.

From below, the others could see Al's body hanging down from the goal funnel while one of his hands jabbed frantically at the control buttons on the belt.

"I said they can be a bit tricky," called Avatar.

Al's muffled voice could be heard from inside the goal funnel though luckily it was impossible to tell what he was saying.

It didn't take long for Al to get the anti-grav belt under control and he was soon hovering around the arena, a short distance above the ground.

"There," he said. "No problem at all. It feels like I have got my legs back ... it is great."

"Right," said Max. "You're almost ready for your first game. There's just one more piece of equipment you need."

Max held out a long pole with a block on one end of it. Sticking out of the block were lots of long, thin spikes.

"What *is* that thing?" asked Al, backing away. "It looks terrible."

"It's called a brush," said Flint. "We use them to scrub the roof."

As the sun sank behind the Mountains of Khan, the Iron City was silhouetted against the evening sky. Lights flickered on all over the city and the engines of mining craft glowed brightly as they buzzed around it like fireflies.

Anyone looking from the windows of those craft might have noticed a small team of robots hard at work, scrubbing the glass of the Eagles' Nest.

"I can't believe it," moaned Crank.

"Now what's wrong?" said Flint.

"When Maximus said there was a team of robots that cleaned the roof, I didn't think he meant *this* team."

"Stop moaning and keep scrubbing," said Flint. "If the glass isn't cleaned in time the fans won't be able to see what's happening and the game will be cancelled."

"But the glass is filthy," complained Al. "This could take us all night."

"That's right," said Flint. "Sometimes it takes even longer than that. So stop moaning and get cleaning. If we're lucky we should be finished in time for the start of the game."

"Who are we playing against?" asked Torch.

"The Metrocity Dynamos," said Avatar. "Flint's old team. That's why he's even grumpier than normal."

"I thought it was us he did not like," said Al.

"No," said Avatar. "He's always grumpy before a game but playing the Dynamos makes him worse."

"If it bothers him that much," said Al," he should stop playing."

"Stop playing!" said Avatar. "He couldn't stop playing even if he wanted to – none of us can.

Anyway, Flint has always been a powerball player and he'll probably keep playing until he gets destroyed in a game."

"What was that about being destroyed in a game?" asked Crank, dropping his brush. "I thought you said there was nothing to worry about."

"I didn't want to worry you," said Avatar. "But it's true ... most powerball players end up getting destroyed in a game."

"Well thank you *very* much," said Crank. "You could have told us this before we started scrubbing the roof. We came here to be stars. Not to get destroyed in a game. Come on guys ... we're going."

"But we has not finished da roof," said Grunt, "and Max said he wants it to sparkle."

"Forget about the roof," said Crank. "We're getting out of here."

"You can't go," said Avatar, shaking her head. "They won't let you."

"What do you mean, they won't let us?" said Crank.

"Like I said," replied Avatar, "we can't stop playing even if we want to."

"But that's ridiculous," said Torch. "Powerball is only a game, after all."

"Not here it isn't," said Flint. "It's like they say … once an Iron City Eagle, always an Iron City Eagle. The Iron City can be a great place to live but people work very hard and the only real fun they get is watching the powerball games. So the Iron City Mining Federation make sure that there are always games for them to watch."

"But robots get hurt playing powerball," said Al.

"Yeah," said Flint. "That's what they like about it. They watch us get bashed up and destroyed instead of worrying about themselves getting bashed and destroyed."

"Well, we didn't come here for that," said Crank.

"We came looking for Robotika … a safe place for old robots. A place where robots can be free to live their lives in peace."

"I came looking for Robotika too," said Avatar. "And I've found out something really important about it."

"What's that?" asked Crank excitedly.

"No one knows where it is," said Avatar. "Now come on … let's get this roof finished."

"I can't believe Maximus didn't tell us about this before," said Torch.

"It's not his job to tell you things like that," said Avatar. "His job is to keep the powerball games going without it costing the city too much money."

"That's right," said Flint. "He goes out looking for pathetic old robots. Useless, desperate pieces of junk that he finds wandering through the mountains or across the Wastelands. He tells them they are going to be big stars and then brings them here to be destroyed."

"But we're not useless, desperate pieces of junk," complained Crank.

"Of course you're not," said Flint, reassuringly. "But Maximus still convinced you to come here, didn't he?"

"But Maximus seemed so nice," said Al. "I cannot believe he would do such a thing to another robot being."

"Oh, he is nice," said Avatar. "But Maximus is just trying to survive like the rest of us."

"It wasn't always like this," said Flint. "When I came to the Iron City everything shone like new. The Iron City Eagles were a real team and the players were treated like stars."

"What happened to it then?" asked Torch.

"The humans all left," said Avatar.

"Dat should be a good fing," said Grunt. "Without da softies messing fings up, da robots can do what dey like."

"It was good at first," agreed Flint. "But now the whole city is run by robots. Things break down and don't get repaired. The place is falling apart."

"Why doesn't everyone leave then?" asked Torch.

"Where would they go?" said Flint. "Robotika?"

"Yes!" cried Crank. "They could go to Robotika."

"And where's that then?" asked Flint.

"Well," admitted Crank, scratching his head, "we're not quite sure."

"That's why they stay here," said Flint. "As bad as the Iron City might be … it's their home. This *is* their Robotika."

"Well it certainly isn't mine," said Crank. "Robotika is a peaceful place where robots are free. It has tall towers and robot palaces that shine in the sun … it's not a rusty old city where robots worry about being destroyed in silly games."

"You don't have to get destroyed you know," said Flint. "I've been playing all my life and I've not been destroyed yet."

"Well that is very reassuring," said Al. "But we have not been playing all our lives so what will happen to us?"

"I'm sure you'll be fine," said Avatar, frowning at Flint. "Now let's get this roof finished so that we can go and prepare for the game."

7

Crank, Al, Torch and Grunt stood with Flint and Avatar on the circular disk that would soon be taking them up to the powerball dome. Between them stood Scamp, decorated with bright yellow pom-poms and streamers.

"Poor Scamp," growled Grunt. "He looks ridiculous."

"I think he looks cute," said Avatar, smiling.

"He's a botweiler," said Grunt. "He's not meant ta look cute."

From above, they could hear the crowd cheering as a loud fanfare boomed from the speakers. Above all the noise came the voice of Maximillion Verm –

the Iron City Eagles official commentator.

"Returning for tonight's game we have two of your favourite Iron City Eagles – Flint Armstrong and the awesome Avatar – but tonight you'll see a new Iron City Eagles team. With four new players they'll be tougher and smarter than any team you've ever seen."

As the crowd roared in appreciation, the floor slowly started to rise and the four friends got their first glimpse of the powerball dome fully powered up and ready for a game.

Giant vid-screens set into the walls at either side of the dome gave close-up shots of the teams as well as showing the game score. The walls themselves shimmered with power, making them almost transparent so the players and the spectators could see each other.

"Just look at them," said Crank, staring at the crowd. "There's thousands of them … and they've all come to see us play."

"Come to see us get trashed, you mean," said Torch. "We must be mad."

The crowd roared in delight and the cheering grew even louder as Maximillion introduced each of the new team members in turn.

"**Crank the Crusher,**" said Maximillion.

Crank's face appeared on the giant vid-screen and the crowd cheered in response.

"I'm not a crusher," said Crank.

"**Al the Annihilator,**" boomed Maximillion's voice.

"Ha!" laughed Crank. "And you're certainly not an annihilator."

"**Torch the Terminator, and Grunt the Grinder,**" said Maximillion.

"I isn't a grinder," said Grunt. "I fink I is more of a basher."

"I think you're right," agreed Crank. "But Grunt the Basher doesn't sound as good, does it."

"I do not think any of them sound good," said

Al. "He is making us sound very nasty."

"I think that's the whole idea," said Torch. "And it might not be such a bad idea either … just look at the other team."

The Metrocity Dynamos stood facing them as they came up into the powerball dome.

"They do not look very friendly at all," said Al, looking at the row of players.

"There's something strangely familiar about them though," said Crank,

scratching at a piece of flaking paint on his head.
"I'm sure I've seen them before."

"They are Regulators," said Torch. "Like the
robots we saw in the recycling plant."

"That's it!" cried Crank. "They're Regulators."

"We can not play against Regulators," said Al.
"They are nasty, vicious, cruel robots that do not
care about anyone."

"That's why I left the Dynamos," said Flint.
"The team was bought by the Metrocity Security
Force and they decided to have only Regulators
on the team. Not any old Regulators though …
only the really nasty ones that were too dangerous
for normal security work."

"Oh great," said Crank. "Things can't get much
worse than this, can they."

While Maximillion Verm introduced the
visiting team and the spectators booed and
stamped their feet, Avatar gathered the Iron City
Eagles together.

"These players are more interested in taking you out than in scoring goals, but remember … they can only touch you if you are holding the ball – so pass it quickly."

"That's right," said Flint. "And don't forget to power it up."

"Power it up?" said Al. "What do you mean, power it up?"

"Don't say that Max didn't tell you about powering up the ball," said Avatar.

The four friends looked at each other blankly and shook their heads.

"Oh great," groaned Flint.

"Does it make much difference?" asked Torch.

"It's the difference between a ball and a power-ball," said Avatar. "Without powering it up, the ball is just a heavy metal ball. But when you power it up it becomes a powerball."

"I see," said Crank, nodding his head. "So what does that mean?"

"It just means that it goes a little bit faster and bounces a little bit more," said Avatar.

"It also means that if you catch it without using your power-glove you will lose your hand," said Flint.

"Lose your hand?" cried Crank.

"Er ... yes," said Avatar. "And you probably don't want it to hit your head either."

"Or your body," added Flint.

"That's right," said Avatar. "So whatever you do, once the ball has been powered up, only touch it with the hand that's wearing the power-glove."

As Avatar was busy explaining about the power-ball, the music came to an end and Maximillion Verm called the two teams together.

"That's Maximus again, isn't it," whispered Crank.

"I think so," replied Al. "But he is wearing a ridiculous hat and a long coat."

Maximillion's face appeared on the vid-screens

at either side of the powerball dome and the crowd fell silent, listening to what he had to say.

"**Tonight's game between the Iron City Eagles and the Metrocity Dynamos is proudly brought to you by the Iron City Mining Federation,**" boomed Maximillion's voice from the loudspeakers.

"**Let's hope it's an exciting game with lots of fair play.**"

On saying that, Maximillion winked at the crowd and they roared back in appreciation.

"Did you see that?" said Crank. "He winked. He knows it's not going to be a fair game."

"It looks fair to me," said Grunt. "Dare is six of dem and six of us. Dat's fair."

"Actually there will only be five of us," said Avatar. "Each team has one reserve player that can come on if one of the others gets injured. That means one of you will need to go and sit in the reserve box."

The four friends looked up to where Avatar was pointing and saw two boxes set into the wall. A Regulator had already taken a seat in one box but the other was empty.

"Grunt isn't sitting in no stupid box," said Grunt. "I is playing da game."

Crank and Al looked at each other for a moment then both made a dash for the safety of the reserve box.

"I'll go!" yelled Crank, pulling Al's arm.

"No!" cried Al. "I will go. It would be a shame for you to miss the game."

"I think Torch should go," said Avatar, stopping Crank and Al in their tracks. "He is older than the rest of us and it might be a good idea to bring him on in the second half of the game.

"Now the rest of you get in your positions … the game's about to begin."

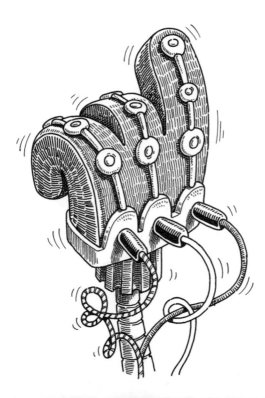

A loud CLANG rang out around the Eagles' Nest as the ball was fired into the air.

"**And the game has begun,**" announced Maximillion Verm over the loudspeakers. "**Let's see who gets to the ball first, shall we?**"

Crank looked up, trying to work out where the ball had gone, but there was no sign of it anywhere. Then, one of the Metrocity Dynamos made a sudden leap into the air and he spotted it. Just before the robot's hand could close around the ball it was snatched from its grasp by Avatar, as she gracefully somersaulted through the air and came to land directly beneath the goal funnels.

"And the Iron City Eagles are in a position to score, with their captain taking control of the ball," announced Maximillion.

Avatar was about to throw the powerball into the goal funnel when she was sent flying. One of the Dynamos had crashed into her, sending the powerball spinning into the air towards the wall.

Crank watched as Avatar rolled across the floor before quickly springing back to her feet.

"Stop him!" yelled Avatar, pointing at the Dynamo that had just knocked her over and was now chasing after the ball.

Crank raced after the robot and barely had time to think about what he was doing as he dived forwards, grabbing the robot's legs as it grabbed the ball. It wasn't until he was being dragged across the floor behind it that Crank thought how strange it was to be chasing a Regulator – especially after he'd spent so much time running away from them when they'd been in the recycling plant.

"Crank is bravely hanging on as the Dynamos attacker struggles to keep control of the ball," came Maximillion's voice. "**Will Crank be able to slow the big robot down or will the— Oh, that's got to hurt.**"

One moment Crank was gripping the Regulator's leg and the next minute he was in a tangled heap, sliding down the far wall. He'd only got a brief view of the bottom of the Regulator's foot as it smashed into his face then everything had gone dark for a moment.

When Crank opened his eyes he found Flint peering down at him.

"Are you all right?" asked Flint. "Looks like you've had your circuits shaken a bit there."

Crank nodded. "I'm all right," he said. "It'll take more than one Regulator to finish me off."

"Good!" said Flint, as he dashed after the ball. "That's the spirit. But you'd better get up before one of them jumps on you."

Crank looked up to see one of the Regulators running towards him. It took a leap into the air and then came straight down, feet first, towards him.

"Arghh!" screamed Crank and just managed to roll out of the way as the Regulator's feet crashed down where he'd been lying.

"Hey!" cried Crank. "I didn't have the ball."

"Oh dear," said the Regulator with an evil grin. "I didn't notice that."

"I bet you didn't," huffed Crank, and turned to walk away. Crank had only taken a couple of steps when he fell flat on his face and felt a heavy weight press on to his back.

"Oops," laughed the Regulator as it stepped on Crank and walked back towards the middle of the powerball dome. "That was a nasty trip you just had."

That's it, thought Crank. *They're not pushing me around like that.* Getting to his feet, he put his head down and charged at the Regulator's back as it walked away laughing. But before he'd got halfway there a hand reached out and picked him up.

"What is you doin'?" asked Grunt, holding Crank up in the air. "Don't you remember what da captain said?"

"What?" said Crank, his legs still running in the air.

"She said you can only get dem if dey've got da ball," said Grunt. "So dat's what we'll do."

"All right, all right," said Crank. "But I've had enough of Regulators pushing me around."

"Come on," said Grunt, "let's get back to da game."

Before the two friends had a chance to get back to the game there was a loud THUB, followed by the sound of a horn.

"What does that mean?" asked Crank.

"It means the Metrocity Dynamos have scored a goal while you two were chatting," said Flint. "Now come on ... we need to play as a team if we're going to win this game."

A second loud CLANG told the players the ball had been fired back into play and there was a rush of movement at one side of the powerball dome as Avatar leaped into the air to catch it.

One of the Regulators jumped after her but Avatar leapfrogged over it, landed on the floor and passed the powerball across to Flint.

"Wow!" said Crank. "She's amazing."

Flint charged forward towards the goal funnels,
hoping to level the score, but found his way
blocked by two more of the Dynamos. Stepping
quickly to one side, he threw the ball back over
his head towards Crank.

"Go Crank!" shouted Flint, ducking as one

of the Dynamos flew over his head and landed on the floor.

Crank reached out and caught the ball in one hand then froze as he saw two of the other Regulators charging towards him down the middle of the powerball dome. The curved wall was right behind him so he couldn't move any further back, and there wasn't enough room to run between the two charging robots.

"It looks like Crank is about to be steam-rollered," announced Maximillion over the loud-speakers. "This game could get nasty."

The crowd cheered and roared, sensing that the game was about to get more exciting.

"Pass!" cried Avatar, waving her arms in the air on the left.

"Throw it," shouted Flint jumping up and down on the right.

Crank looked at his two Iron City Eagle team-mates but couldn't decide what to do. Both of them had Dynamos leaping around next to them so he couldn't make a clear pass. Their goal minder was hovering right in front of their goal funnel so there was no chance of him scoring.

The two Regulators were getting closer by the second and Crank felt as though his feet had been welded to the floor.

"**Caboom!**" said the voice of Maximillion over the loudspeakers, cruelly predicting what was about to happen.

The two charging robots were only a few steps
away from him when Crank remembered what
Flint had said. *Don't forget to power it up …*

Gripping the ball tightly in his power-glove,
Crank used his other hand to give it a twist.
Beneath his hands, the two halves of the ball
turned smoothly and clicked into a new position.

Instantly, the ball let out a soft hum and began
to glow with a bright red light.

"**POWERBALL!**" came Maximillion's voice, the
words echoing around the dome.

The two charging Regulators skidded to a
halt and stared at the ball in Crank's hand –

wondering what he was going to do with it.

Then he spotted Grunt.

His friend was thundering towards him, behind the Regulators, and right away Crank knew what to do.

"Catch!" said Crank and tossed the powerball towards the two Regulators. It wasn't a big throw that would go past them or a powerful throw that could knock them off their feet. It was the sort of throw that anyone could catch …

... and the two Regulators reached out and caught the ball as it passed between them.

"Mine!" they shouted together – each of them gripping one half of the glowing ball in their power-gloves.

"Mine!" growled Grunt and he landed on the two Metrocity Dynamos, sending them crashing to the floor beneath the weight of his huge body-slam.

The power drained from the powerball, returning it to its normal colour as it rolled out of the Regulators' outstretched hands and across the floor towards Crank.

Flint, Avatar and the two remaining Regulators were already running across the powerball dome towards the ball, but Crank got there first.

Scooping the ball up in his hand, Crank jumped over Grunt and the two flattened Regulators and made a dash towards the goal funnels.

As he got closer, the Dynamos goal minder hovered down towards him, trying to make it harder for Crank to score.

Crank dived forwards and gave the powerball a second twist as he flew through the air. The two halves of the ball smoothly clicked into position again – but this time the ball glowed bright blue as it started to hum.

"**BOUNCEBALL**," came Maximillion's voice over the loudspeakers.

Just before he hit the floor, Crank threw the glowing powerball down in front of him. The ball touched the floor and shot back up into the air like a rocket.

THUB.

The sound of the powerball going into the goal funnel came just as Crank hit the floor and as the goal horn blared out, Maximillion's voice came over the loudspeakers again.

"**And the Iron City Eagles even the score with**

a blistering goal from newcomer Crank the Crusher," said Maximillion. "It's one goal each in this battle between two great teams."

"That was fantastic," said Flint, picking Crank up off the floor. "Where did you learn moves like that?"

"I've no idea," said Crank. "It just came to me."

"Well, keep them coming!" said Flint. "We could use a few more goals like that."

As the ball was fired back into play, the two Dynamos Grunt had landed on were getting shakily to their feet. Amazingly they weren't out of the game but they'd certainly been slowed down a bit. Crank just hoped they wouldn't give him any more trouble.

The powerball landed neatly in Avatar's gloved hand as it came down from the top of the dome. She rushed towards the goal funnels, hoping to put the Iron City Eagles ahead, but found her way blocked by one of the Dynamos.

Turning to find someone to pass to, Avatar spotted Flint running round the edge of the dome trying to shake off a Regulator that was hot on his heels.

"Pass," shouted Flint, waving his arms in the air.

Without slowing down, Avatar gave the power-ball a twist, powering it up, and threw it across to Flint.

The red glowing ball was safely in Flint's gloved hand before the word *powerball* had even been announced.

Dodging to one side, Flint broke away towards the centre of the powerball dome and aimed for the goal. Still powered up, the ball was just a red streak in the air as it shot past the Dynamos goal minder and into the waiting funnel.

THUB.

The horn echoed around the arena announcing the Iron City Eagles' second goal of the game, and was quickly replaced by the sound of a buzzer.

"With score at two goals to one, the first quarter of the game comes to an end with the Iron City Eagles taking the lead," said Maximillion, his grinning face appearing on the vid-screens.

After only a couple of minutes' break, the powerball was fired into the air and the second quarter of the game started.

This time the ball came straight towards Crank, who caught it easily in his hand. Seeing one of the Regulators coming towards him, Crank quickly threw the ball over its head and into Flint's waiting power-glove.

Flint started running straight away but the Regulator turned quickly and smashed into him, sending him crashing into the wall at the side of the dome. Flint slid down the wall, grabbing for the ball as it fell from his gloved hand.

"**Flint's down**," announced Maximillion, "**but it's not over yet. This veteran player doesn't let go of the ball that easily.**"

But as Flint got back to his feet a second Regulator charged straight into the front of him and a third one hit him from behind.

"Now **that's** what you call a metal sandwich," said Maximillion, as Flint collapsed to the floor.

There was an ear-splitting crunch as one of the Regulators jumped on to Flint's back and the powerball rolled out of his outstretched hand.

"**Flint's down again and the Dynamos have control of the ball**," said Maximillion.

Hovering around the Iron City Eagles' goal funnel, Al flew down to meet the advancing Dynamos players but there was nothing he could do to stop the ball once it had been powered up. The ball shot past his power-glove and into the goal behind him with a resounding THUB.

"That brings the Metrocity Dynamos even with the Iron City Eagles at two goals each," said Maximillion.

Running across to the far end of the powerball dome, Crank and Avatar barely heard the score being announced. Flint was still lying on the floor and small wisps of blue smoke were snaking from round his joints.

"You're next," growled one of the Regulators, pointing at Crank as it walked away from Flint's motionless body.

"It looks like Flint's out of the game," said Maximillion as the powerball was fired back into the air.

Crank didn't see the powerball whizzing past his head and he hardly even noticed as the Metrocity Dynamos scored their third goal and the sound of the horn echoed around the arena. He just couldn't believe what had happened.

Crank stood and stared as the game carried on around them. He felt as though his feet were bolted to the floor and he couldn't move.

Without anyone to stop them, the Metrocity Dynamos scored their fourth goal, but still Crank didn't move.

Avatar was on the floor, kneeling down next to Flint, hoping to see some sign of life, but the old powerball player lay perfectly still.

Grunt picked up Flint's broken body and held him in his arms.

"'He's gone," said Grunt. "Dis is just scrap metal now … Flint is gone."

"GONE?" cried Crank. "But he was one of the best powerball players in the galaxy, he can't have just *gone*."

"It's the way he would have wanted it," said Avatar sadly. "Come on … It's up to us now."

"What do you mean, it's up to us!" cried Crank. "We can't carry on playing without Flint. Without him the Iron City Eagles are finished."

"I know," said Avatar. "But we have to carry on.

It's all part of the game."

"This isn't a game!" said Crank. "It's crazy."

"Players come and players go," said Avatar. "But the game goes on. We'll have to bring on Torch, our reserve player."

But looking up at the reserve box, Crank couldn't see Torch. A door had been opened behind Torch's seat and there was no sign of the old Fire and Rescue robot anywhere.

"Where is he?" said Crank. "I can't believe he'd just sneak away like that. I thought he was our friend."

"It looks like the Iron City Eagles reserve player has gone missing," announced Maximillion. **"It's going to be hard for them to catch up with the Dynamos with only four players."**

And as if to prove what Maximillion had said, there was a loud THUB from the middle of the powerball dome as the Metrocity Dynamos scored another goal.

"Nothing can stop the Dynamos now," announced Maximillion. "I think this could be the end of the Iron City Eagles."

"Oh no it's not," growled Grunt, and stepped in front of one of the Dynamos, *accidentally* tripping the robot up.

The Regulator got back to its feet and snarled at Grunt, swinging a fist at him that landed right on his chin.

"Is dat da best you can do?" asked Grunt, picking the robot up by one of its legs.

A second Regulator leaped into the air, hoping to crush Grunt the same way it had crushed Flint earlier, but it didn't have a chance. Using the first Regulator as a bat, Grunt swatted it away and sent it crashing into the wall.

While Grunt was busy with two of the Regulators, the audience cheered with delight and other fights broke out around the powerball dome, all thoughts of scoring goals forgotten.

One of the Dynamos had pinned Crank down and was busy trying to bash his head against the floor while Avatar wrestled with it from behind.

Even Scamp, the botweiler, had somehow managed to join in and had one of the Regulators pinned against the wall with his huge paws.

Only the two goal minders weren't fighting.

Al and the Metrocity Dynamos goal minder were hovering in front of the scoreboard vid-screens, watching what was going on.

The match score and close-ups of the in-game action had been replaced by a news programme. The screen was filled with smoke and flames, and small fire drones could be seen busily spraying foam down into what looked like a lift shaft.

As everyone in the powerball dome caught sight of what was happening on the vid-screen, the crowd fell silent and the fighting gradually stopped.

Even Grunt stopped bashing the Regulator on its head and joined everyone else in watching the big vid-screen.

"What's going on?" asked Crank.

"Looks like there's a fire in one of the legs of the city," said Avatar. "It happens quite often — usually triggered by a gas explosion. The city loses lots of good mining robots because the fire drones just can't handle the fires."

"Well dat one seems to be doin' all right," said Grunt, pointing at the screen.

As they watched, a figure appeared through the wall of fire and smoke. Over its shoulder it was carrying two other robots that it had rescued from the lift shaft below.

At the sight of the rescued mining robots a huge cheer went up around the Eagles' Nest and Crank, Al and Grunt stared at the screen in disbelief.

"That's Torch," cried Crank. "What's *he* doing there?"

"Looks like he's rescuing miners and putting out fires," said Avatar.

Crank and the others watched as Torch busily directed the fire drones, pulled the trapped mining robots up from the shaft and extinguished the fire. As the last of the flames died away another huge cheer went up from the crowd in the Eagles' Nest.

"Wow!" said Crank. "I knew he was good but I didn't know he could do that."

"He *is* a Fire and Rescue robot," said Al. "What did you *think* he did?"

"Oh, aren't you the clever one," said Crank.

"Of course," said Al. "After all, I am one of the latest home maintenance robots and have been fitted with many improved intelligence and memory circuits that you older—"

"Oh!" cried Crank. "So you're calling me old and stupid, are you?"

"Are you two going to stand here arguing," interrupted Avatar, "or are we going to get out of here?"

"What about Maximus?" asked Crank. "Won't he stop us?"

"The Iron City Eagles are finished now that Flint's gone," said Avatar. "Maximus is probably getting out of here while he's got the chance."

Avatar led Crank, Al and Grunt through a door in the side of the powerball arena and up a narrow staircase.

"Where are we going?" asked Al.

"I thought you wanted to find Robotika," said Avatar.

"Robotika!" said Crank. "Is it up here?"

"Of course not," said Avatar. "But this leads up to the roof and that's where Maximus leaves his ship."

"Not the *Terrapin?*" said Crank and Al together.

"I'm afraid so," said Avatar. "It may be an old wreck, but it's the only way we'll ever get off this city."

By the time they reached the door at the top of the stairs, Scamp was already there waiting for them. The robots burst through the door and out on to the open roof of the Eagles' Nest. At the far end, away from the glass, stood the *Terrapin*, its engines rumbling as it prepared for lift-off.

"Wait for us," shouted Avatar, racing across the roof and on to the boarding ramp.

Before the others had reached the bottom of the ramp the *Terrapin* was lifting off and moving out over the edge of the roof.

"Come on," yelled Avatar, reaching out from the bottom of the ramp.

Still wearing the anti-grav belt, Al easily hovered on to the *Terrapin*, but Crank had to take a running jump with Grunt and Scamp close behind him. The ramp rattled and shook beneath their weight and Crank staggered backwards, almost falling off the edge. Avatar reached out just in time, grabbing Crank's arm and pulling him to safely.

As the *Terrapin* started moving further away from the powerball dome, another figure appeared on the roof.

"Look," said Al. "It is Torch."

"Come on!" yelled Crank. "Jump!"

"No," shouted Torch, shaking his head. "I'm not coming."

"What do you mean, you're not coming?" shouted Crank. "We're going to Robotika ... Come on, you can make it."

"Who will put out the fires if I leave?" said Torch. "They need me here."

"But we can't go without you," said Crank.

"I'm getting too old for all this travelling round," said Torch. "Putting out fires and rescuing people is what I do best ...

perhaps I've found my Robotika right here."

As the *Terrapin* started to gain height and leave the Iron City behind it, the four friends watched as Torch gradually disappeared from sight.

"Don't worry," said Avatar. "He'll be fine. Now, which way should we go?"

"I don't really know," admitted Crank. "Hey ... who's flying this thing?"

"Welcome aboard the *Starship Terrapin*," came a familiar voice over the loudspeakers. "I'm Maximus Bullwart and I'll be your pilot for today ... Robotika, here we come."

After leaving the Iron City behind it, the *Starship Terrapin* broke through the clouds leaving a thick trail of smoke behind it. Then there was a loud bang from somewhere outside the ship and an alarm started wailing.

The door to the flight deck opened and Maximus came running out.

"What's happening?" said Crank.

"Nothing to worry about," said Maximus. "Just a little engine trouble."

"Engine trouble!" cried Crank. "What sort of engine trouble?"

But Maximus didn't answer. He disappeared through another door which closed behind him with a clunk … then there was a muffled bang, followed by a loud hiss.

"I think he has gone," said Al, examining the door that Maximus had passed through.

"Gone!" said Crank. "What do you mean, gone?"

"This was an escape pod," said Al. "And it looks like Maximus has escaped in it."

"But who's flying the ship?" said Crank.

"No one," said Avatar, rushing on to the flight deck. "And we're going down."

The End

CRANK

AL

AVATAR

GRUNT

book 1

The Tin man

The giant metal claw hanging above the bath had swung round and grabbed Crank round the waist. Crank used all his strength to try and get free from the claw's steely grip … but it was no use. He found himself being carried up and over the side of the bath.

Crank just had time for a final look at his friends. He could hardly believe his eyes. The other robots were sitting there as if nothing was happening. Even Al didn't seem concerned. *Some friends*, he thought, as the claw started to lower him towards the liquid.

Bubbles erupted fiercely below him and clouds of foul-smelling gas rose into the air. Crank was sure the bath was full of acid and he was about to be dissolved.

"Arghhhhhh!" he screamed, as the steel claw lowered him into the bath, "I'm melting …"

book 5

The Ghost Sea

"Right," said Crank. "Now what?"

"This is the easy part," said Avatar. "Now we crash."

The *Starship Terrapin* hit the ground with a joint-shattering crunch and its nose dug into the earth, ploughing a long trench in the sea bed. A shower of sand and dried mud flew into the air as it went along.

Inside the ship, smoke filled the air and sparks flew from the control panels and rained down on the four friends. Then the vid-screen on the wall exploded, showering them all with glass.

Scamp, the botweiler, let out a loud metallic howl as the lights blinked out. The control room was plunged into darkness but still the ship sped along, shaking and rattling as it ploughed through the earth, hitting rocks and boulders, before eventually coming to a shuddering halt.

"Well," said Al, unfastening his safety belts, "that could have been worse."

DAMIAN HARVEY

lives in Blackpool with his wife and three daughters, their four cats, a horde of guinea pigs, a tank full of fish and a quirky imagination.

He loves music, movies, reading, swimming, walking, cheese and ice cream – but not always at the same time.

Before realising how much fun he could have writing and making things up he worked as a lifeguard, had a job in a boring office and once saved the galaxy from invading vampire robots (though none of these were as exciting as they sound).

Damian now spends lots of time in front of his computer but loves getting out to visit schools and libraries to share stories, talk about writing and get people excited about books.